This book belongs to

_____

CECILY PARSLEY'S NURSERY RHYMES

BEATRIX POTTER
ILLUSTRATED BY
ALLEN ATKINSON

AN ARIEL BOOK

BANTAM BOOKS
TORONTO   NEW YORK   LONDON   SYDNEY

CECILY PARSLEY'S NURSERY RHYMES
A Bantam Book
December 1983

Design: Iris Bass
Art Direction: Armand Eisen

Acknowledgment: The illustrator would like to thank Hal Hochvert and Anne Greenberg for their fine work on the production of this book, with special thanks to the editors Ron Buehl and Lu Ann Walther

ISBN 0-553-15229-7

Bantam Books are published by Bantam Books, Inc. Its trademark, consisting of the words "Bantam Books" and the portrayal of a rooster, is Registered in U.S. Patent and Trademark Office and in other countries. Marca Registrada, Bantam Books, Inc., 666 Fifth Avenue, New York, New York 10103

Printing and binding by
Printer, industria gráfica S.A.   Provenza, 388   Barcelona-25
Depósito legal B. 29084-1983
PRINTED IN SPAIN
0   9   8   7   6   5   4   3   2   1

The art is dedicated
to my godson,
Taarak

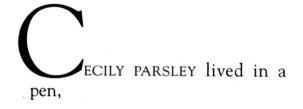

CECILY PARSLEY lived in a pen,

CECILY PARSLEY'S NURSERY RHYMES

CECILY PARSLEY'S NURSERY RHYMES

And brewed good ale for gentlemen;

Gentlemen came every day,

Till Cecily Parsley ran away.

CECILY PARSLEY'S NURSERY RHYMES

CECILY PARSLEY'S NURSERY RHYMES

GOOSEY, goosey, gander,
Whither will you wander?

CECILY PARSLEY'S NURSERY RHYMES

Upstairs and downstairs,

CECILY PARSLEY'S NURSERY RHYMES

CECILY PARSLEY'S NURSERY RHYMES

And in my lady's chamber!

CECILY PARSLEY'S NURSERY RHYMES

THIS pig went to market;

CECILY PARSLEY'S NURSERY RHYMES

CECILY PARSLEY'S NURSERY RHYMES

This pig stayed at home;

CECILY PARSLEY'S NURSERY RHYMES

This pig had a bit of meat;

CECILY PARSLEY'S NURSERY RHYMES

CECILY PARSLEY'S NURSERY RHYMES

And this pig had none;

This little pig
cried
Wee! wee! wee!

CECILY PARSLEY'S NURSERY RHYMES

I can't find my way home.

CECILY PARSLEY'S NURSERY RHYMES

PUSSY-CAT sits by the fire;

CECILY PARSLEY'S NURSERY RHYMES

How should she be fair?

CECILY PARSLEY'S NURSERY RHYMES

In walks the little dog,
    Says "Pussy! are you there?"

CECILY PARSLEY'S NURSERY RHYMES

"How do you do, Mistress Pussy?
  Mistress Pussy, how do you do?"

CECILY PARSLEY'S NURSERY RHYMES

CECILY PARSLEY'S NURSERY RHYMES

"I thank you kindly, little dog,

I fare as well as you!"

CECILY PARSLEY'S NURSERY RHYMES

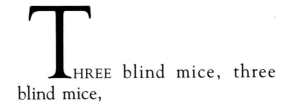

THREE blind mice, three blind mice,

CECILY PARSLEY'S NURSERY RHYMES

See how they run!

They all run after the farmer's wife,

CECILY PARSLEY'S NURSERY RHYMES

And she cut off their tails with a carving
knife,

CECILY PARSLEY'S NURSERY RHYMES

CECILY PARSLEY'S NURSERY RHYMES

Did ever you see such a thing in your life

CECILY PARSLEY'S NURSERY RHYMES

As three blind mice!

CECILY PARSLEY'S NURSERY RHYMES

Bow, wow, wow!
Whose dog art thou?

CECILY PARSLEY'S NURSERY RHYMES

"I'm little Tom Tinker's dog,
    Bow, wow, wow!"

CECILY PARSLEY'S NURSERY RHYMES

CECILY PARSLEY'S NURSERY RHYMES

WE have a little garden,
A garden of our own,

CECILY PARSLEY'S NURSERY RHYMES

And every day we water there

CECILY PARSLEY'S NURSERY RHYMES

The seeds that we have sown.

CECILY PARSLEY'S NURSERY RHYMES

We love our little garden,
    And tend it with such care,

CECILY PARSLEY'S NURSERY RHYMES

CECILY PARSLEY'S NURSERY RHYMES

You will not find a faded leaf

Or blighted blossom there.

CECILY PARSLEY'S NURSERY RHYMES

Ninny nanny netticoat,
In a white petticoat,

With a red nose,—
The longer she stands,
The shorter she grows.

CECILY PARSLEY'S NURSERY RHYMES